W9-ALN-068

A Dragon

on the

Doorstep

written by **Stella Blackstone**

illustrated by **Debbie Harter**

There's a dragon on the doorstep,
Do you think he wants to play?

Let's lock him in the closet,
Then let's run away!

There's a crocodile in the closet,
Don't go inside!

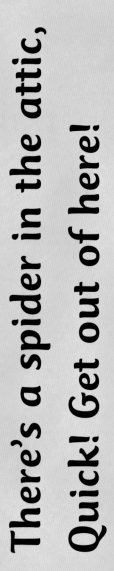

There's a spider in the attic,
Quick! Get out of here!

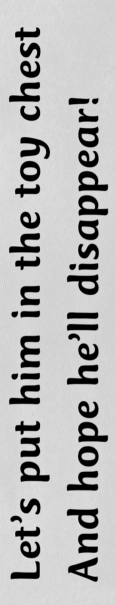

Let's put him in the toy chest
And hope he'll disappear!

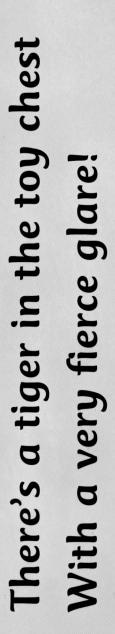

There's a tiger in the toy chest
With a very fierce glare!

Let's chase him to the bedroom
And tell him to stay in there!

There's a big bear in the bedroom,
With the most enormous paws!

Let's hide him in the laundry
And make sure we shut the doors!

There's a lion in the laundry,
Have a look and see!

Let's shut him in the garage
And lock it with the key!

There's a gorilla in the garage
And all the others too!

Everybody has escaped!
Watch out or they'll catch you!

What a lot of animals!
Let's all go outside.
Then we can play another game
And everyone can hide!

For Sarah, with much love — S. B.

For Eva, Yoyo and Luke — D. H.

Barefoot Books
2067 Massachusetts Ave
Cambridge, MA 02140

This book was typeset in Bokka and Mercurius Medium
The illustrations were prepared in watercolor, pen and ink and crayon on thick watercolor paper

Graphic design by Barefoot Books, Bath
Color separation by Grafiscan, Verona
Printed and bound in China by South China Printing Co. Ltd

This book has been printed on 100% acid-free paper

1 3 5 7 9 8 6 4 2

Library of Congress Cataloging-in-Publication Data
Blackstone, Stella.
A dragon on the doorstep / written by Stella Blackstone ; illustrated by Debbie Harter.
p. cm.
Summary: Easy-to-read, rhyming text describes a game of hide-and-seek among the animals in a child's home.
ISBN 1-84148-227-7 (hardcover : alk. paper) [1. Hide-and-seek--Fiction. 2. Animals--Fiction. 3. Stories in rhyme.]
I. Harter, Debbie, ill. II. Title.
PZ8.3.B5735Dr 2005
[E]--dc22
2004028587

Barefoot Books
Celebrating Art and Story

At Barefoot Books, we celebrate art and story with books that open the hearts and minds of children from all walks of life, inspiring them to read deeper, search further, and explore their own creative gifts. Taking our inspiration from many different cultures, we focus on themes that encourage independence of spirit, enthusiasm for learning, and acceptance of other traditions. Thoughtfully prepared by writers, artists and storytellers from all over the world, our products combine the best of the present with the best of the past to educate our children as the caretakers of tomorrow.

www.barefootbooks.com